Under the Microscope: Backyard Bugs

GRASSHOPPERS

PowerKiDS press
New York

Suzanne Slade

To my sister-in-law, Wendy

Published in 2008 by The Rosen Publishing Group, Inc.
29 East 21st Street, New York, NY 10010

First Edition

Editor: Joanne Randolph
Book Design: Julio Gil
Photo Researcher: Nicole Pristash

Photo Credits: Cover, pp. 1, 5, 7, 9, 13, 17, 19, 21 © Shutterstock.com; p. 11 © Dennis Kunkel Microscopy, Inc.; p. 15 © istockphoto.com/Roy van Zijl.

Library of Congress Cataloging-in-Publication Data

Slade, Suzanne.
  Grasshoppers / Suzanne Slade. — 1st ed.
      p. cm. — (Under the microscope: backyard bugs)
  Includes index.
  ISBN-13: 978-1-4042-3820-6 (library binding)
  ISBN-10: 1-4042-3820-4 (library binding)
  1. Grasshoppers–Juvenile literature. I. Title.
  QL508.A2S59 2008
  595.7'26—dc22
                                                2006037190

Manufactured in the United States of America

Contents

Step into Your Backyard

On a warm summer day, you might find a surprise when you step into your backyard. Pop! Something suddenly springs up out of the grass. It may even jump over your head! What is this mighty jumper? Take a closer look, and you will discover the grasshopper.

Grasshoppers like to live in sunny places with lots of plants. The place where plants and animals live is called a **habitat**. Your backyard is a great habitat for grasshoppers because they can hide in the grass, warm themselves in the sun, and eat plants that grow near the ground.

A grasshopper uses its strong back legs to jump. It can jump high enough to touch a basketball net.

4

Part of a Group

Grasshoppers belong to a group of **insects** called the Orthoptera. Crickets are also part of this group. Orthopterans have many things in common. They have long legs, a large head with flat sides, and two pairs of wings. When these insects are at rest, their top pair of wings lies straight across their back. The top wings cover two thin wings that are used for flying.

Orthopterans also have a strong mouth for chewing. Some people think these insects are pests because they often travel in large groups and eat crops.

We can tell orthopterans apart from other insects by looking at their head. Do you see the flat sides on the head and the large, strong mouthparts?

Kinds of Grasshoppers

There are about 23,000 kinds of grasshoppers in the world. In North America, there are 1,000 different kinds of grasshoppers. Grasshoppers like warm weather. They do not live near the North Pole or South Pole, where it stays cold all year.

Most grasshoppers are short horned or long horned. A short-horned grasshopper has short **antennae**, while the antennae on a long-horned grasshopper are very long. One of the smallest grasshoppers in the world is the pygmy grasshopper. This gray and brown insect is ¼ to ½ inch (.6–1.3 cm) long. The American grasshopper is brown and yellow and measures around 2 inches (5 cm).

This long-horned grasshopper is called the walking leaf grasshopper. Looking like a plant leaf helps the grasshopper stay safe from animals that want to eat it.

A Grasshopper's Body

Did you know that a grasshopper has five eyes on its head? It has two large eyes, called **compound eyes**. Each compound eye has hundreds of tiny lenses that see movement. A grasshopper also has three small eyes between the compound eyes. These small eyes see darkness and light.

Grasshoppers are known for their long, strong legs. The powerful **muscles** in each back leg allow a grasshopper to jump about 20 times its body length. All six of a grasshopper's legs are found on its **thorax**. The long back part of its body is the **abdomen**.

This is a special, close-up photo of a grasshopper's head. You can see one of the compound eyes here.

Exoskeleton

Antennae

Compound eye

Mouth

Magnification: x 5

11

What a Life!

The grasshopper begins its life as a tiny white egg. When this egg **hatches**, in the spring, a small baby insect, called a nymph, crawls out. At first, the nymph is almost all white. A few hours later, colors appear on the nymph and it looks like a small adult grasshopper without wings.

Nymphs spend most of their time eating plants. As a nymph grows, it becomes too large for its skin. When this happens, it **sheds** its outer skin. A nymph will shed five or six times before it becomes an adult grasshopper.

It takes about 40 to 60 days for a nymph to become an adult grasshopper.

It Takes Two

When a male, or boy, grasshopper is ready to **mate**, he makes a special sound. This sound calls a female, or girl, grasshopper to him. About 14 days after mating, a female lays her eggs. She uses a tube in her abdomen to place her eggs.

Long-horned grasshoppers lay eggs on plants. A short-horned grasshopper digs a hole in the ground and lays 25 to 150 eggs in the soil. Then she makes glue and mixes it with dirt. This hardens to form a cover around the eggs.

This long-horned grasshopper's abdomen is full of eggs. She is ready to lay her eggs on a plant.

A Feast Fit for a Grasshopper

Do you think you could eat a pile of food that weighs as much as you do? A grasshopper eats its weight in food every day! Grasshoppers have tiny sticks on their mouth, called palpi, which help them taste food.

Most grasshoppers are not picky eaters. Short-horned grasshoppers eat just about anything that is green. These plant eaters like grass, leaves, and different crops. Long-horned grasshoppers dine on plants and insects. They often eat bugs that are already dead. Their mouth moves side to side as they chew on tiny, tasty insects.

A large group of grasshoppers can eat a whole field of corn or wheat. This grasshopper sits on a wheat plant.

17

Enemies of the Grasshopper

Grasshoppers are a tasty insect that many animals eat with just one bite. Skunks, foxes, coyotes, mice, and raccoons all feed on the juicy grasshopper. Birds, such as owls and bluebirds, eat grasshoppers, too. To stay safe, grasshoppers hide under plants or jump away. If they are caught, grasshoppers can shoot a brown juice from their mouth, which scares their enemies.

Grasshopper eggs and nymphs are tasty treats, too. Fly larvae, which are worms that turn into flies, often eat tiny grasshopper eggs. Lizards, mice, and beetles eat grasshopper nymphs.

This lucky spider has caught a grasshopper. Spiders are an important part of the backyard habitat, too.

A Grasshopper's Song

On a quiet night, you may hear the sound of grasshoppers calling out. Grasshoppers may sing to call females, scare away males, or tell other grasshoppers about danger. A grasshopper does not push air out of its mouth to sing, like people do. In fact, it does not even breathe through its mouth. Grasshoppers breathe through holes on their thorax and abdomen.

Grasshoppers make noise by rubbing body parts together. A short-horned grasshopper has pointed files on its back legs. It chirps by rubbing these sharp files over a wing. The long-horned grasshopper makes sounds by lifting its wings and rubbing them together.

This grasshopper might sing to find a mate, to keep itself safe, or to talk to other grasshoppers.

Discover the Grasshopper

Listen for the song of a grasshopper in your backyard. Watch for its colorful wings as it flies through the air. Grab a net and catch one of these high jumpers. Be careful not to hurt your backyard neighbor, though.

Look closely at the bug you have caught. Is the grasshopper red, green, yellow, black, or brown? Does it have long or short antennae? Antennae help a grasshopper feel what is near. Place the grasshopper on your hand and it will use its antennae to learn about you. Soon it will hop from your hand back to its home in your backyard.

Glossary

abdomen (AB-duh-mun) The large, back part of an insect's body.

antennae (an-TEH-nee) Thin, rodlike feelers on the head of certain animals.

compound eyes (KOM-pownd EYZ) The larger eyes of bugs, which are made up of many simple eyes.

habitat (HA-beh-tat) The kinds of land where an animal or a plant naturally lives.

hatches (HACH-ez) Comes out of an egg.

insects (IN-sekts) Small animals that often have six legs and wings.

mate (MAYT) To come together to make babies.

muscles (MUH-sulz) Parts of the body that make the body move.

sheds (SHEDZ) Gets rid of an outside covering, like skin.

thorax (THOR-aks) The middle part of the body of an insect. The wings and legs come from the thorax.

Index

A
abdomen, 10, 14, 20
American grasshopper, 8
antennae, 8, 22

C
compound eyes, 10
crickets, 6
crops, 6, 16

H
habitat, 4

I
insect(s), 6, 8, 12, 16, 18

L
leg(s), 6, 10, 20
lenses, 10

M
muscles, 10

N
North Pole, 8
nymph(s), 12, 18

O
Orthoptera(ns), 6

P
palpi, 16
pests, 6
pygmy grasshopper, 8

S
skin, 12
South Pole, 8

T
thorax, 10, 20

Web Sites

Due to the changing nature of Internet links, PowerKids Press has developed an online list of Web sites related to the subject of this book. This site is updated regularly. Please use this link to access the list:
www.powerkidslinks.com/umbb/ghop/